KT-163-905

For Constantin – ST

For Ellen – HS

We Have Lift-Off © Frances Lincoln Limited 2013
Text © Sean Taylor 2013
Illustrations © Hannah Shaw 2013

The moral rights of Sean Taylor and Hannah Shaw have been asserted

First published in Great Britain and in the USA in 2013
This early reader edition published in Great Britain in 2013 by
Frances Lincoln Children's Books,
74-77 White Lion Street, London, N1 9PF
www.franceslincoln.com

All rights reserved

ISBN 978-1-84780-477-8

Printed in China

1 3 5 7 9 8 6 4 2

Created in consultation with language and literacy
development specialist, Prue Goodwin.